For Henry Douglas and all our favorite friends.

Special thanks to Samir and Violette.

Also, Beth. Nothing good happens without you.

Text and illustrations copyright © 2020 by Curt Luthye

ISBN 978-1-7348665-0-6

G & C Stories

skunkandrat@gmail.com
www.facebook.com/skunkandrat
www.instagram.com/skunk_and_rat

Tell Me a Reason Why
A Skunk and Rat Story

Written by Graysen Luthye and Curt Luthye
Illustrated by Justice Lanclos

Rat, do you love me?

I do, Skunk.
I really do.

Hmmm, let's see ...

You aren't afraid to be yourself.

You throw fantastic birthday parties.

You make up songs spontaneously and sing them to me.

You are always ready to dance.

You love a good challenge and don't stop until you figure it out.

You like to twirl in dresses.

You listen when I want to tell a story.

You stop to smell the flowers.

You love
to take walks
with me.

You're always ready with an interesting fact you just discovered.

Did you know reindeer eyes turn blue in the winter?

You paint great pictures.

You're kind and don't leave people out.

Come play with us, Jacob!

You're my friend.

Thanks, Rat. I needed that.

No problem, Skunk.

Yes?

I love you, too.

Graysen Luthye is a 10-year-old girl with curly locks and a lot of energy. She likes to cook, dance, hike, and go on adventures with her dog, Jacob. Her favorite things to do with friends are building forts, going camping, playing at the beach, and exploring new places—anywhere, really, as long they are together. She has never met a book she wouldn't read, but her favorite author is J.K. Rowling. Originally from San Diego, California, she currently lives with her mom and dad in Baltimore, Maryland.

Curt Luthye is Graysen's dad. He enjoys taking walks, spending time in nature, and meeting new people. His favorite people are kids because they remind us to approach life with curiosity, joy, and laughter. His favorite things to do with friends are playing games, sharing meals, and having good conversations. His favorite author is C.S. Lewis. He has lived in and visited countries all over the world, but his favorite place to be is home with his family.

Justice Lanclos is an illustrator currently residing in Baltimore, Maryland. Influenced by both American artistic traditions and Japanese traditions, she loves the use of texture and big doe eyes. A fiend for a good dose of magic, she hopes to transport viewers with her work, whether that be by evoking memories or widening perspectives. To find more of her work or to hire her for your next project, go to www.momentsofjustice.com.

CPSIA information can be obtained
at www.ICGtesting.com
Printed in the USA
LVHW072230020620
657267LV00030B/547